SANTA MOUSE
Makes a Christmas Wish

 LITTLE SIMON

An imprint of Simon & Schuster Children's Publishing Division
1230 Avenue of the Americas, New York, New York 10020
First Little Simon paperback edition September 2021
Copyright © 2021 by Michael Martin Brown
Written by W. Harry Kirn
Illustrated by Robert McPhillips
Based on the character of Santa Mouse created by Michael Brown

For information about special discounts for bulk purchases, please contact Simon & Schuster Special Sales at 1-866-506-1949 or business@simonandschuster.com.
The Simon & Schuster Speakers Bureau can bring authors to your live event. For more information or to book an event contact the Simon & Schuster Speakers Bureau at 1-866-248-3049 or visit our website at www.simonspeakers.com.
Designed by Claire Torres
Manufactured in China 0621 LEO
10 9 8 7 6 5 4 3 2 1
ISBN 978-1-5344-3799-9
ISBN 978-1-5344-3800-2 (eBook)

SANTA MOUSE

Makes a Christmas Wish

Based on the character created by
Michael Brown

LITTLE SIMON

New York   London   Toronto   Sydney   New Delhi

Long ago there was an empty house.
It was the home of tiny Santa Mouse.

At the North Pole, very far away,
Santa and his elves worked night and day.

On Christmas Eve when Santa flew his sleigh,
Santa Mouse joined in to help him on his way.

But what about the other days each year?
How could this clever mouse spread Christmas cheer?

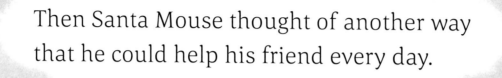

Then Santa Mouse thought of another way
that he could help his friend every day.

Helping him would be a dream come true
so Santa Mouse knew what he had to do.

Making gifts for all girls and boys,
bikes and dolls and lots of toys!

The mouse filled every wish—Santa's elves were surprised by his special presents, each one personalized.

But when he had finished, it was clear to all
that his tiny paws had made the toys too small.

"Everything came out all wrong," he cried.
The elves agreed, it couldn't be denied.

If *making* toys did not come easily,
could *wrapping* them be a possibility?

It was a task that looked like lots of fun
as long as every gift was neatly done.

There were papers colored red and green and gold
and bows for every package, bright and bold.

He wrapped each gift with all the care he could
and added name tags just the way he should.

But it is true, as every mouse would say
that long tails surely can get in the way.

When he was finished, it was a sorry sight.
Each gift was wrinkled, not a one was right!

Then Santa entered with a "Ho! Ho! Ho!"
He'd never seen his little friend so low.

"If you would like to help us celebrate,
I see a Christmas tree to decorate."

Cheerfully the mouse took his advice.
Lights and tinsel would look very nice.

He loved this task so much, he didn't stop
'til he had placed a golden star on top.

The tree shone brightly, and it didn't take long
before Santa and his elves had joined in song.

But the happiest voice that there ever has been
came from Santa Mouse, who had finally fit in.